Maisy Goes on Holiday

Lucy Cousins

WALKER BOOKS
AND SUBSIDIARIES
LONDON · BOSTON · SYDNEY · AUCKLAND

The holidays have come at last!
Oooh! How exciting!
Maisy is packing her blue bag
to go to the seaside.
Sunhat, camera, books.
What else will she need?

Maisy's taking the train and Cyril is coming too. There he is, buying the tickets. The station is so busy today.

Puff,
puff!

The train pulls
away from the platform.

Maisy does some colouring.
Cyril chooses some snacks.

Everyone looks for their tickets when the conductor comes.

Can you see the sea?

At the hotel Maisy and Panda bounce on the bed. Then it's time to unpack and go to...

the beach!

Splash! Maisy loves
to go right in.

Splish! Cyril likes to paddle.

There's so much to do on the beach –

collect shells,

build castles,

run about and play for hours and hours.

At the beach café,
Maisy has an ice cream

and Cyril has a
fruit juice special.

Then they write postcards. Cyril writes to Charlie. Maisy writes to her friend Dotty. "Our first day at the seaside was lovely," she tells her.

And it's lovely staying in the hotel.
Sleep well, Maisy.
Sleep well, Cyril.

Have a
happy holiday!